Baby Moses

Sky Pony Press books may be purchased in bulk at special discounts for sales promotion, corporate gifts, fund-raising, or educational purposes. Special editions can also be created to specifications. For details, contact the Special Sales Department, Sky Pony Press, 307 West 36th Street, 11th Floor, New York, NY 10018 or info@skyhorsepublishing.com.

Sky Pony® is a registered trademark of Skyhorse Publishing, Inc.®, a Delaware corporation.

Visit our website at www.skyponypress.com.

10 9 8 7 6 5 4 3 2 1

Manufactured in China, July 2016
This product conforms to CPSIA 2008

Library of Congress Cataloging-in-Publication Data is available on file.

Cover design by Brian Peterson
Cover photo credit Brendan Powell Smith

Print ISBN: 978-1-5107-1266-9
Ebook ISBN: 978-1-5107-1267-6

Editor: Julie Matysik
Designer: Brian Peterson
Production Manager: Joshua Barnaby

Baby Moses
THE BRICK BIBLE for Kids

**Brendan
Powell Smith**

Sky Pony Press
New York

God's chosen people, the Israelites, had come to Egypt to escape a famine in their homeland. After living in Egypt for a very long time, the Israelites had become numerous and successful, and the whole land was full of them.

The new Pharaoh, the king of Egypt, was afraid of the Israelites, because there were so many of them. He said to his people, "We must be wise and do something to prevent the Israelites from becoming more powerful than us!"

So Pharaoh decided to make the Israelites slaves to weaken them. The enslaved Israelites were forced to do hard work for the Egyptians all day long.

But the Israelites continued to have many children, and they became even more numerous. So Pharaoh announced, "From now on, the Israelites may only have daughters. Every son that is born to an Israelite family must be thrown into the river."

At this time there was an Israelite woman named Jochebed who was married to Amram. They had a son named Aaron and a daughter named Miriam. Now Jochebed was pregnant and soon her family would have another child.

When the time came and Jochebed gave birth, the baby was a fine looking boy. Aaron and Miriam now had a little baby brother.

Jochebed carefully kept her newborn son hidden so that the Egyptians would not discover him and throw him in the river.

But she knew she could not keep him hidden forever,
so after three months she took a basket and sealed it
so it would not leak.

Then she brought the baby down to the marshes at the edge of the Nile River. She placed her baby inside the basket and put the basket into the river.

Standing at a distance, Miriam kept watch over her brother in the basket, waiting to see what would happen to him.

That same day the princess of Egypt came down to the river to bathe.

She spotted the basket floating in the marshes and wondered what it was. She told one of her servants to go and get the basket, and bring it to her.

When she looked inside the basket the princess saw
a crying baby boy.

"This must be the child of one of the Israelites,"
said the princess.

She felt pity for him and did not want to put the
baby back in the river.

Just then, Miriam approached the princess and said, "Would you like me find an Israelite woman to nurse the child and care for him?"

The princess replied, "Yes, go and do so."

Miriam went off to find her mother and take her to the princess.

When the princess met Jochebed, she said to her, "Take this child and nurse him. I will pay you to take care of him for me."

And so Jochebed's little son was returned to her arms. She brought him home, nursed him, and took care of him for as long as he was a baby.

When the child was old enough, Jochebed brought
her son to Pharaoh's palace.

She returned the boy to Pharaoh's daughter, and the princess adopted him as her own son.

The princess said, "I will name him Moses, because I brought him out of the water."

Moses grew up in Egypt, and one day when he was
an adult, God spoke to him from a burning bush and
chose him to become the leader of the Israelites.

With God's help, Moses freed the Israelites from
slavery and brought them out of Egypt by splitting
the Red Sea so the Israelites could escape.

Later on a mountaintop, God gave Moses laws for the Israelites to follow, known as the Ten Commandments. And in the years ahead, Moses would lead his people to the holy land of Israel.

Activity!

Can you find these ten brick pieces in the book?
On which page does each appear?
The answers are below.

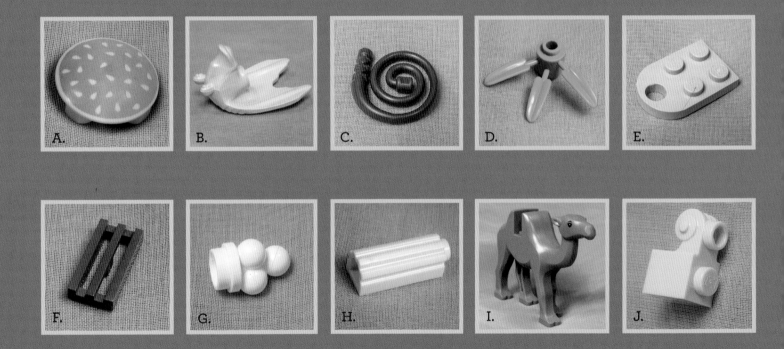

A.

B.

C.

D.

E.

F.

G.

H.

I.

J.